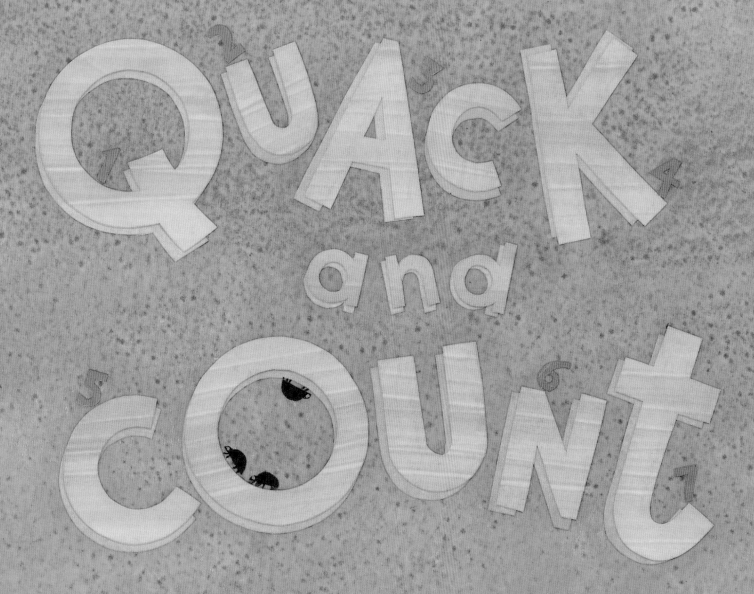

QUACK and COUNT

KEITH BAKER

Clarion Books
An Imprint Of HarperCollinsPublishers
Boston   New York

The Library of Congress has cataloged the hardcover edition as follows:

Baker, Keith. 1953– Quack and count/Keith Baker. p. cm. Summary: Seven ducklings take a rhyming look at addition. 1. Addition—Juvenile literature. 2. Seven (The number)—Juvenile literature. 3. Ducks—Juvenile literature. [1. Addition. 2. Seven (The number). 3. Ducks. 4. Counting.] I. Title. QA115.B35 1999 513.2'11—dc21 98-7924 ISBN 0-15-292858-8 ISBN 0-15-205025-6 pb

The illustrations in this book are cut-paper collage.
The display lettering was hand cut by Keith Baker.
The text type was set in Goudy Sans Bold.
Color separations by Bright Arts Ltd., Hong Kong
Printed in China
Production supervision by Sandra Grebenar and Pascha Gerlinger
Designed by Keith Baker and Judythe Sieck
SCP   30 29 28 27 26 25 24
4500847060

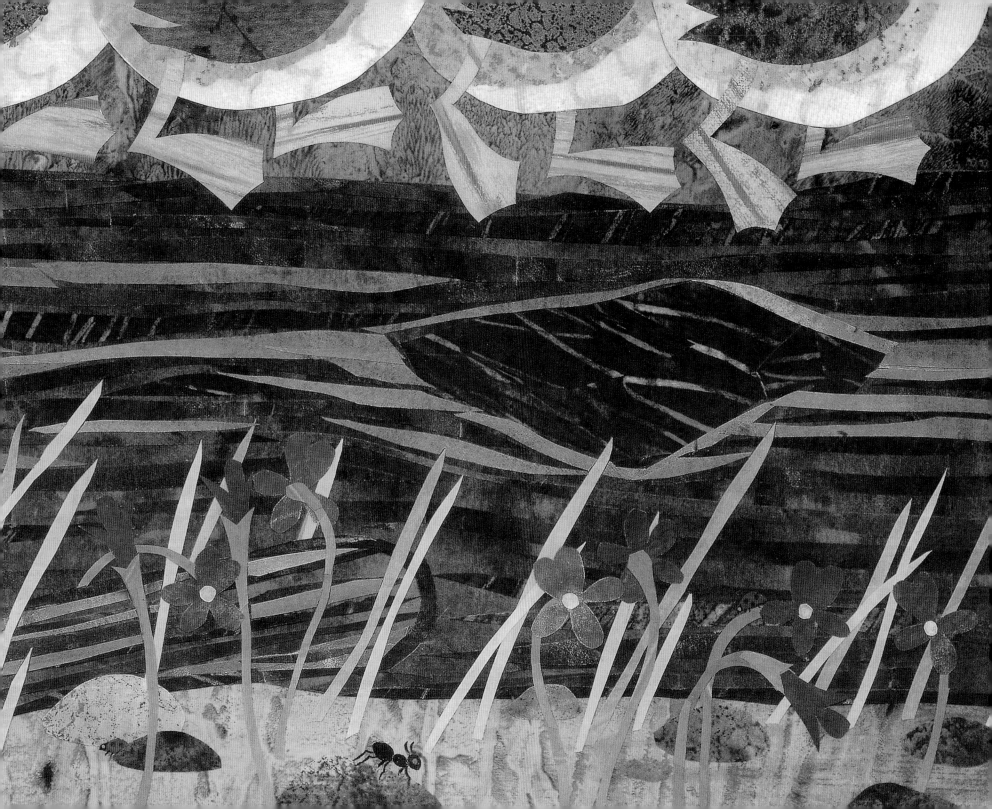

7 ducklings in a row
Count those ducklings as they go!

Slipping, sliding, having fun
7 ducklings, 6 plus 1

7 ducklings, 5 plus 2
Playing games of peekaboo

Chasing busy bumblebees
7 ducklings, 4 plus 3

7 ducklings, 3 plus 4
Quack-quack-quacking on the shore

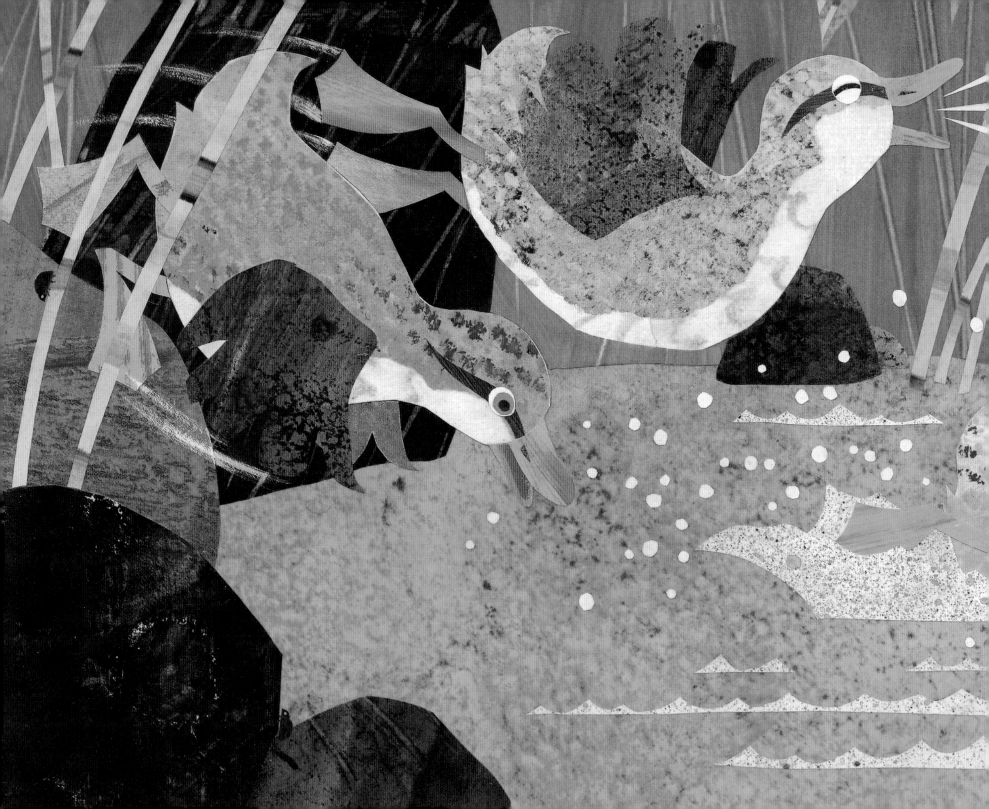

**Splashing as they leap and dive
7 ducklings, 2 plus 5**

7 ducklings, 1 plus 6
In the water playing tricks

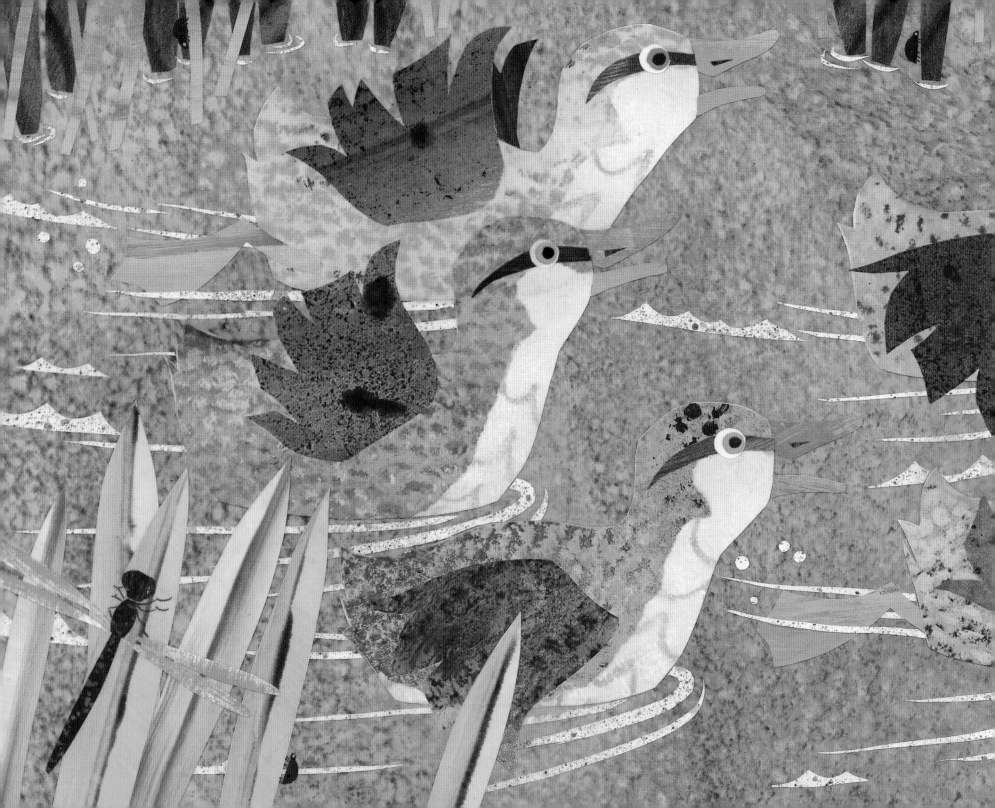

**Paddling, flapping, reaching high
7 ducklings start to . . .**

FLY !

**Up and up into the sky—
Good-bye, ducks . . .**

good-bye,

good-bye.